Al Katar 

Other Books of Fiction

Pensacola Sharks
Captain Scratch Vol. 1-3
The Amazon Effect
The Last Warrior
Gator Restaurant
Country Line
G Corporation
Bus Ride
Meet Black People
Short Stories:
The Monkey
The Drop Off Zone
Third Strike
Stick Man
Education
Call of Duty, Two, Military Park
Call of Duty, G-Corporation
Call of Duty books are comprised of a
series of a lease three, but at this time at
least ten literary works in the making.

CALL OF DUTY
G-CORPORATION

By

AL Katar

ISBN 978-1-957956-58-9 (Paperback)
ISBN 978-1-957956-59-6 (Ebook)

Inquiries and Book Orders
should be addressed to:

Leavitt Peak Press
17901 Pioneer Blvd Ste L #298,
Artesia, California 90701
Phone #: 2092191548

CONTENTS

DISCLAIMER

This is a work of fiction. **Names, characters, business, events and incidents are the products of the author's imagination.** Any resemblance to actual persons, living or dead, or actual events is purely coincidental.
Education News Network
P.O. Box 18116
Pensacola, FL 32523
© 2022

FORWARDS

G-Corporation. The "G" is for Global. G-Corporation represents a new wave of thinking of the United States Government. Turning the management of the Armed Forces over to a private corporate company, to what has been sold to them.

Because of budget cutting, a more effective and economical way of saving money while maintaining a strong military even in war time is the goal.

"K" Troop, 1st battalion, 1st infantry division is one such unit under the control of G-Corporation. This book details this veteran and highly decorated military unit; that is preparing to rotate back to another overseas deployment. Some of the unit's members are on their third deployment in eight years.

The strain on their families is taking its toll. G- Corporation has been in control of the United States Military spending for ten years. The promise cost saving of this joint venture is yet to be fully realized. In other words, "the jury is still out".

THE CHARACTERS

Sergeant Terry, his friends call him "T" is a ten-year veteran making his forth deployment overseas. He is a young, divorced, single man with a two-year-old daughter and baby momma problems.

Sergeant Rice, an eight-year veteran is Terry's next-door neighbor in base housing. Sgt. Rice is a family man with two children, and he is preparing to make his third deployment.

Corporal McGee, a seven-year veteran is a wife and mother of a two-year child making her second deployment.

This diverse group has their own reasons for being in the military. Follow them on their new mission and their relationship with G- Corporation.

CHAPTER I

The Adventure Begins

As the sun pierce through the window of Sergeant Terry's bedroom. With one day left before "T" is to report for a one-year deployment overseas. "T" goes outside to retrieve his newspaper and mail. Back inside as he enjoys his morning cup of coffee, "T" opens a letter from the court system. They inform him that the mother of his child has requested an increase in child support. "T" says "when it rains, it pours". Suddenly there's a knock on the door. "Come in" says "T". It's Sgt. Rice from next door.

Rice says hey man, one day left before "D" day. How do you feel and how's thing's on the home front?

Terry, well my baby momma is cutting up, but things will work themselves out like they always do.

Rice say's "Brother, I've got some bad news for you. I'm not going to be deployed with the unit, because I didn't pass my physical. My blood test came back funny. Good luck "T", I'm out the game for good. See you when you get back."

The next day early in the morning "T" leaves his home, dressed in his military uniform and spit shined boots. As he leaves his driveway a long dark limo stops in front of Sgt. Rice home with a big letter "G" on its side. A man in a dark business suit appears.

After a short drive to the military base, where his unit is station. "T" is directed to a large hanger where other members of his unit are gathered. They greet each other and talk about the mission ahead. In the crowd he sees an old friend Cpl. McGee. Cpl. McGee is one of a hand full of women soldiers in the unit. She says goodbye to her husband and child. After they leaves "T" walk's over to say hello.

Hi McGee, what's happening! Cpl. McGee, I've heard about Rice. Sorry he wants be coming with us, he's a good guy. Do you know where we're going this time? "T" no, your guest is as good of mine; you know that's a secret now days, until we arrive. They will tell us when the time come.

What I do know is we will be going to Mississippi for a month of pre-training, you know a little house to house. G Corporation says it's part of the military good neighbor policy,LOL.

Later that morning the unit boards a C-130 airplane. After arriving in Mississippi, the training was hard and fast, with very little time off. After one month the unit board's a bigger jumbo jet for an 18-hour flight to the Middle East to part's unknown. As they fly over the snow caped mountain of Afghanistan, McGee says at least we know it's not Iraq.

An hour later the plane descends through the clouds to a runway no one on the plane is familiar with. The troops debark into a large hanger to be briefed on their mission and their location.

Their battalion commander is holding a briefing with a large map behind him. Greeting the troops saying, this is Project 5218. Your mission is to stop what we think is a flow of arms through this small township between these two mountains ranges.

We discovered this town by satellite severance a year ago. It's not even on most of the world maps. "K" unit will be the first military unit to ever enter this small town. We've no inside Intel. Our battalion will lock down all roads, trails and check the town for weapons. Your mission starts in the morning at 0400 hours, it's a 30-minute drive by jeep to the town. If there are no questions, remember your training, dismissed. "T" tells McGee to sum it up we are bait, the sacrificial lambs.

CHAPTER II

The Village

Early the next morning "T" is put in charge of the mission. Armed to the teeth and ready for action, "K" troop makes their way to the entrance of the town. The unit is on edge. Based on their pass experience things should be on and popping in a few minutes. As they slowly make their way into the town they see the town's people, they both are very curious of each other. "K" troop at this time fines no enemy contact, but surprisingly to their amazement the town is well put together, sub modern buildings, and an active marketplace.

The people are of all colors and races. A large park with green grass, not unlike any small town in America. Even a basketball court. "T" stations his unit in and around the town. The town is on lockdown! "T" reports on his radio phone to headquarters. "T" makes McGee his assistant on this mission. They both survey the town on foot with a small group of troops ready for action.

They discover the town's people are friendly and helpful. "T" even buys some fruit in the outdoor marketplace.

McGee says to "T" this must be a dream, too good to be true. Suddenly a basketball appears rolling toward them, the team, takes cover. Taking no chances that it might be a bomb, the ball slowing, stops rolling.

McGee says shall we shoot it, to find out what it is. "T" says wait a minute, suddenly a teen-age boy appears and says in broken English. Do you play ball!

A man appears also saying to his son, these men don't have time for playing ball. "T" says wait a minute. Yes, I have time for one game of horse or 21. The game gathers a large crowd with them cheering for both players. After one game "T" and his patrol unit are invited by the boy's father to meet his family, "T" accepts.

As they enter their home, they are impressed by the large numbers of books in the study. An older gentleman has his back to them reading a book. He slowly turns around; and he looks Eastern European.

This is my father, Omar. Mr. Omar speaks prefect English. Welcome to my home. Mr. Omar introduce the rest of his family. This is my wife Susan and my daughter Sarah.

Sarah is a very beautiful young woman. "T" is mesmerized by her beauty. After some small talk, "T" is invited to dinner, he accepts.

During dinner "T" explains a few things about his life back home; and asks Mr. Omar how he ended up in this part of the world?

He explains he was a professor at a major university and got tired of the materialist west. Opportunities came about to tour and write about this part of the world, so I fell in love with the mountains and people and stayed.

I had to learn new ways of living and even bring in a little western technology. One such thing is a small hydroelectric power plant attached to the water fall that you've seen on your way into the village. I have also help create schools for both boys and girls.

Through education my people can make decisions to maintain their independent. "T" says do you support the rebels we're here to fight.

Mr. Omar explain this village has been on a major trade route for centuries. We maintain our independent by not taking sides. If a man asks you for a cup of water, you don't ask him about his politics.

Both men finish their small talk with a better understanding and respect for each other's culture. "T" thanks Mr. Omar for his hospitality and retires for the night on the upper hill side in the forest just outside of the village.

CHAPTER III

"T" and Sarah

The next day while on patrol "T" sees Sarah shopping in the marketplace. He approaches her and proceeds to make small talk. They walk together and she gives him a tour of the township and explains her culture.

Sarah say's you see we do have some modern conveniences. Tell me "T", how long will you be in our village? I don't know, hopefully not long. As they walk and share stories, they become closer.

For the next week, they spend a little time each day together. One day "T" finds the courage to steal a kiss, not knowing how Sarah might react. Sarah says, Father says we must not be afraid to try new things. Good night "T".

Later that night at headquarters. McGee says to "T", I hope you're not losing your focus and edge.

No, I have not, but I do think that I'm in love with Sarah. Suddenly a solider place his hand on "T" shoulder. When he turns to see who it is, he is surprised to see that it is Sgt. Rice.

"T" says man, what are you doing here, I thought you were out the game for a while? Rice, I thought so also. The morning you left; G Corporation came to my home to explain my contract options. When I enlisted, I was not under the old guidelines for getting put out of the military.

Under G-Corporation you have to repay all of the bonus money I took and lose all military benefits. I didn't understand that they control our banking, credit card and all communications back in the States. Even this unit's communications. That's too high of a price for my family to pay in this economy. So, I had to opt back into 1st battalion, so now I'm here, what's jumping brother?

"T" says glad your back anyway. You're assigned to my unit for now. We're moving out in the morning, back to the township.

At mid-day while on patrol walking with Sarah near the village park, suddenly a large explosion hits in middle of the park. T's unit heads for cover, as he shields Sarah from harm. "T" calls HQ with excitement in his voice! We have incoming mortar fire; can you tell where it's coming from? Yes "T" it's from U.S artillery, we are checking our range finder.

Did you not get the word? "T", what word? HQ has orders to ICE the town tomorrow at 0900 with a sub-atomic bomb. "T" races back to HQ to get a better explanation. As he enters the HQ, he is hot under the collar and ready to fight.

"T" this must be a mistake. Battalion Commander says G- Corporation has decided to destroy the town and end the village people support for the rebels. "T" says what rebels, I haven't seen not even one rebel. Commander say, G-Corporation believes, it's more cost efficient to destroy the town rather than pay soldiers to patrol or guard it.

"T", these people are not a threat. They are peace loving people. We have not been attacked, not even one shot against us in two weeks. Sgt. "T" it doesn't matter, G Corp makes the decisions ten thousand miles away.

Your orders "T" are to stand down and clear out of town an hour before the blast at 0800 hours. That's all, you're dismissed. "T" leaves HQ to gather support to stop the bombing with no luck. He even tries to call out on the unit's satellite phone with no success.

G-Corp has shut down all outside phone calls as word spreads around the base of "T" efforts. He is looked upon and treated as a turn coat and traitor. A bad American Soldier, who will not go along with the order to destroy the town.

CHAPTER IV

The Last Day

After finding no support at HQ, "T" goes back to the town and explains to his unit the situation. All are sympathetic, but some are for it and some not.

Cpl. McGee, I am sorry "T", but there's nothing we can do.

Sgt. Rice says, I am with you "T", but you know to fight G-Corp is to lose everything. Some soldiers say it's just a spot on a map. The world won't even miss this town brother.

"T" goes to Mr. Omar and a town meeting is quickly held about the situation. The elders weigh their options and decide to stay. They explain this has been their home for centuries. They know no other place or way of life. If it ends for him in the morning, it's something they can accept.

"T" mind is racing. He asks Sarah to speak to her father, so that he might change his mind to evacuate.

Sarah say's "T" you came ten thousand miles to find the enemy. I think you have found them, or shall I say the corporation you serve.

"T" say's to Sarah, I won't stop trying to stop it. Can you help me? Does your village have a two-way radio or cell phone?

Sarah thinks hard and say's, yes we have a cell phone that someone left behind a few years ago. My younger brother played with it as a toy. I will ask him for it.

Sarah comes back with a real cell phone. The problem is that it's an old model known as a brick, and it has no power.

"T" goes to the professor to ask for his assistance in connecting a power source. They both put their knowledge together and behold. After two hours of hard work the phone lights up and there is a dial tone.

The room is filled with excitement. As "T" dials the phone to his baby mother.

Hello this is the Brown family leave a message at the beep. "T" says, her last name is Potter. I must have dial the wrong number. He dials the number again same answer.

"T" then dials Sgt. Rice's home. Hello this is the Jones residence. I'm having a party, call back later. He dials the number again, same answer. He dials the Pentagon in Virginia, and the phone is picked up to "T" relief. The person says, hi this is DC pizza shop, our slogan is "If you can eat it, We can make it". May I take your order.

"T" finally realizes the cellphone is so old that the numbers on it do not match the new cellular frequencies. The number 2 on his phone is the new number 5 and a number 9 is the new number 4.

With time running out, he has to take his chances and just dials 10 numbers at random.

"T" dials again, this time he hits gold. Randy's Hardware, may I help you? Sir I have an emergency! I am an American soldier overseas. My name is Sgt. Terry K Unit, 1st Infantry, 1st Battalion.

Project 5218 has to be shut down. Do not bomb, no threat. My last 4 of my social is 7291. Call the Pentagon, Whitehouse, FBI or anybody. Right away Sgt. I have your caller ID locked in my phone. I'll do it right away.

I'm a retired veteran myself. Good luck, over and out!

The room bursts into celebration. People are overjoyed. Now they can wait for conformation on a return call.

Suddenly without warning, the phone sparks and catches fire. At this time, you could even hear the air being sucked out of the room, as if all hope was lost.

"T" is disappointed about the phone but remains hopeful.

As the sun rises over the snow caped mountains of the village, still no new orders from HQ. With two hours left before the sub-atomic artillery round is fired.

"T" orders his unit to prepare to move back to HQ. Cpl McGee and Sgt. Rice urge "T" to come with them. He decides to stay with the Village people.

With one hour left his unit heads back to HQ. "T" keeps a Jeep with a radio hoping HQ will not fire with an American in the village. T asks HQ not to fire or give him an extension of time for G- Corp to reconsider, but his request falls on deaf ears.

The village people stay at home today to be with their loved ones. The village is quiet. Fifteen minutes left. Sarah comes out to be with "T". They kiss as if it's their last day together on earth. They hold each other for the final moments.

With five minutes left, HQ gives the order to load the bomb. Two minutes left. "K" unit braces for impact and shockwaves back at HQ.

Thirty seconds left as "T" monitors the countdown over the Jeep radio. Ten, nine, eight, seven, six, five, four three, two, one. The round is fired. It will take another thirty seconds for the round to hit. "T" head is spinning. All he can see is his life pass in front of him without his love's ones and Sarah.

Seconds left, Five, four, three, two, out of know where a man's hand is placed on "T" shoulder. "T" turns around and see's the same man in a dark suit from G-Corp that was at Sgt. Rice home.

Go home, back to your unit Sgt. Terry, the bomb will not explode. The experiment is over. G-Corporation just wanted to know what and how soldiers will react under extreme pressure.

"The Jury is Still Out"

The End

ABOUT THE AUTHOR

AL Katar was born a baby of the Civil Rights Movement in the mid 1950's. A child of the 60's. A man of the 70's and a storyteller of the 21st t century, who hasn't forgotten the great writers of the past. He writes in the action, suspense, drama, comedy and the everyday "just be real with me story" genre. From stories titled "The Last Warrior", "Gator Restaurant", "Third Strike", "Drop Off Zone", "The Monkey", "Pensacola Sharks", "Meet Black People" just to name a few and also a bonus feature "Education,

The Sitcom", Katar consider himself to be a transfer writer. Katar to his knowledge is the only writer to publish a three book trilogy on the black pirate "Captain Scratch". He is looking for representation in the film, book and entertainment industry. Katar hopes to build a meaningful relationship and partner with progressive Hollywood studios to maximize sales of a number of his books to be made into movies. He believes with the right management team and investment network the sky is the limit. Some wise person once said only when a writer is stretched and has suffered, that writer will become better. Katar is ready and willing to suffer and to be stretched all the more. See Amazon/AL katar/ Books.

SYNOPSIS

Call of Duty
G-Corporation

The more things change the more they stay the same. This novel in some ways illustrates man and women kind, continuing battle, within the human consciousness to obey or disobey; his or her own Interpretation of being an asset or non-asset in the ever-ending search for a greater humanitarian presence on the earth.

AL Katar

AL Katar at Work

Credits/Contributors

Education News Network (ENN)

Of Pensacola, Florida

Mr. Cedric (Cid) Langham

ENN Vice President Chicago, Illinois

Publicist

Patricia Ann Pryor

Country Line Music.Com

Song "My Heart" written by AL Pryor

Three Broke Comics.Com

Writing Staff

Scratch Kids Products

Bug Tubes

Spencer For Hire Graphics of Pensacola,

Florida, for front and back cover.

Avonbuynow.com